BOBBY AND THE BROCKLES

Other Avon Children's Books by
Adele Faber *and* **Elaine Mazlish**

BOBBY AND THE BROCKLES GO TO SCHOOL

ADELE FABER and ELAINE MAZLISH
BOBBY AND THE BROCKLES

Illustrated by HENRY MOREHOUSE

AVON BOOKS ◆ NEW YORK

BOBBY AND THE BROCKLES is an original publication of Avon Books. This work has never before appeared in book form.

AVON BOOKS
A division of
The Hearst Corporation
1350 Avenue of the Americas
New York, New York 10019

Library of Congress Cataloging in Publication Data:
Faber, Adele.
    Bobby and the Brockles / Adele Faber and Elaine Mazlish ;
illustrated by Henry Morehouse.
        p.   cm.
    Summary: Two little men called Brockles help Bobby to see how to get along with his family and friends by expressing his feelings and working out compromisses.
    [1. Emotions—Fiction. 2. Conduct of life—Fiction.
3. Interpersonnal relations—Fiction.]   I. Mazlish, Elaine.
    II. Morehouse, Henry, ill.   III. Title.
PZ7.F1112Bo   1994   93-42283
[Fic]—dc20   CIP

First Avon Books Trade Printing: September 1994

AVON TRADEMARK REG. U.S. PAT. OFF. AND IN OTHER COUNTRIES, MARCA REGISTRADA, HECHO EN U.S.A.

Printed in the U.S.A.

ARC   10   9   8   7   6   5   4   3   2   1

To all the boys and girls
who would like a visit from the Brockles

Chapter 1

A Surprise Visit

Once again everyone was mad at Bobby Babbit. And once again he was mad at everyone. Just today he'd had a fight with his mother, a fight with his father, and a fight with his friend Sam.

And none of it was his fault. Just because he wanted to wear his red shirt, his mother had a fit. She said, "Absolutely not! It's too dirty. You wore that shirt yesterday and the day before and the day before that." And just because he said a bad word under his breath and grabbed the shirt away from her and put it on anyway, she yelled at him and made him take it off.

What happened with his sister Abby wasn't his fault either. He told her to stay away from his new bicycle, but she rang the bell, so he punched her. He didn't punch her that hard. She didn't have to cry so loud. And she didn't have to go running to Daddy. And Daddy didn't have to take her side and blame him.

And the fight he had with Sam
certainly wasn't his fault. Bobby
tried to tell him the rules for Go
Fish, but Sam wouldn't listen. He
wanted to play it *his* way, with *his*
rules, and his rules were dumb.
Sam was a big baby.

That night Bobby couldn't fall
asleep. He rolled over on one side.
He rolled over on the other side.
He lay flat on his stomach and then
flat on his back, and he still

couldn't sleep.

Then he heard the rain. Not just a light pitter-patter rain, but a heavy splish-splash rain. The wind began to blow. It blew so hard it banged the tree branches up against the window. It blew so hard it made the curtains twist and turn and fill with air like big colored sails. It blew so hard it blew the rain right into Bobby's room. Bobby leaped out of bed and ran to the window to shut it. Just as he did, he heard a crack of thunder and saw a flash of lightning. Quickly he jumped back under the covers and pulled them over his head.

That's when he first heard
their voices. They were arguing
with each other.

"I told you to move faster.
That kid almost slammed the
window on my toe!"

"I couldn't move faster. The
wind was blowing too hard."

"Then you should've let me go
first. I'm soaking wet. *Kerchoo!*
See, I'm catching cold because of
you."

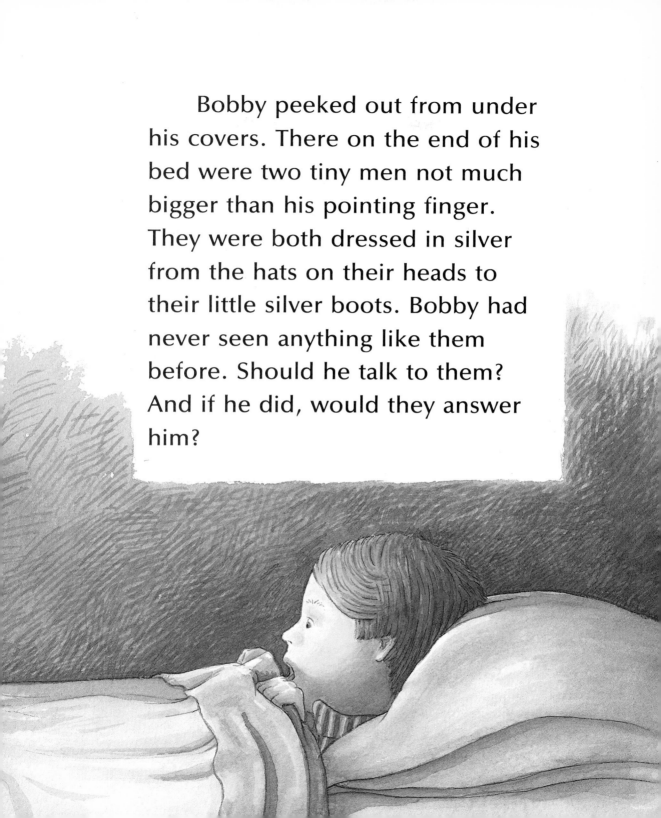

Bobby peeked out from under his covers. There on the end of his bed were two tiny men not much bigger than his pointing finger. They were both dressed in silver from the hats on their heads to their little silver boots. Bobby had never seen anything like them before. Should he talk to them? And if he did, would they answer him?

"Who are you?" Bobby whispered.

"I'm Murry," said the taller one, taking off his silver cape and shaking off the droplets of water.

"I'm Groot," said the short fat one between sneezes.

"But *what* are you?" Bobby asked.

"We're Brockles," they said together.

"Where do you come from?"

"The Brocklesphere."

"Where's that?"

"Questions, questions!" Groot harumphed and blew his nose noisily into a little handkerchief. "You tell him, Murry.

8

I gotta dry off."

Murry climbed up onto Bobby's knee and sat down. "The Brocklesphere is far, far away," he said, pointing to the sky.

"How far?" Bobby asked.

"Above the clouds and below the moon."

"How did you get from there to here?"

"We rode down to earth on a raindrop."

"But how will you get back?"

"We'll walk back on a moonbeam."

Groot harumphed again. "Who . . . what . . . where . . . how!" he growled impatiently. "What's the difference *how* we got here? What's important is *why* we're here. You didn't ask *why*. Don't you want to know why?"

Before Bobby could answer,

Groot said, "It's a Brockle's job to help children with problems, and you, kid, have a big, big problem."

"But it's not my fault," said Bobby. "Everyone is always picking fights with me for no reason."

"Exactly!" Groot shouted, getting even more excited. "And you're always losing those fights, aren't you? Don't you want to know how to win? Well, I'm going to show you how. I'm here to teach you how you can get *your* way."

"No, no, no," said Murry. "Bobby doesn't need to learn how to get his way. He needs to learn how to get along. And that's not easy."

"He needs to learn how to get tough," Groot snapped, "and that's not hard. Don't worry, kid. Stick with me. I'll tell you just what to do."

Murry shook his head. "You'd better think twice before you do what Groot tells you."

Groot laughed, a funny little *heh-heh-heh* laugh, and did a double somersault on the end of the bed.

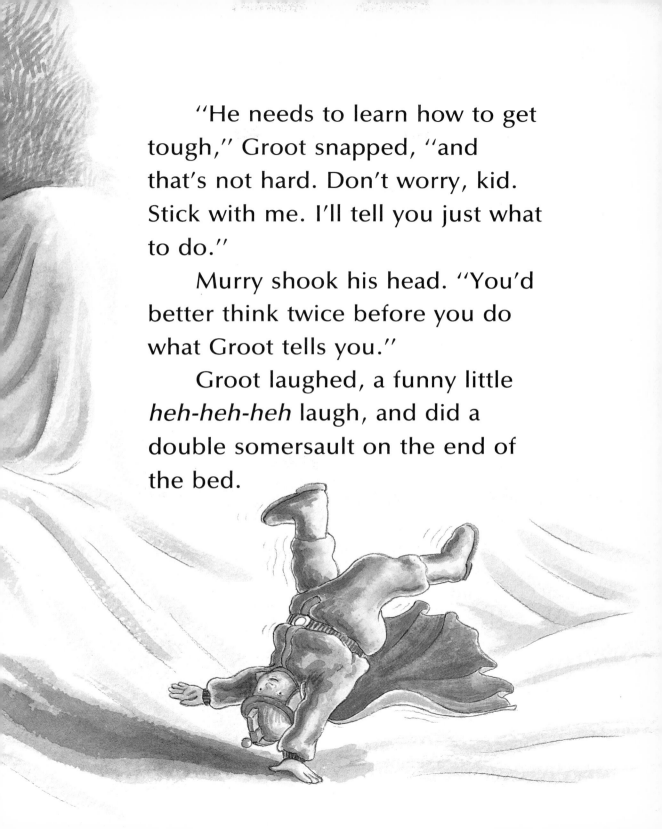

Bobby felt all mixed up. "I don't know who to listen to," he said.

"Me, of course," Groot said, puffing up his chest and pointing to himself. "Me! Me! Me!"

"Listen to both of us," said Murry. Then he cleared his throat and recited:

> *"When in trouble,*
> *When in doubt,*
> *Just slow down,*
> *Think it out.*
> *Make sure you hear*
> *Each point of view,*
> *Then decide*
> *What's right for you."*

Bobby thought about what
Murry said. There was something
he wanted to ask him, but
suddenly he felt very tired. He
could hardly keep his eyes open.
As he drifted off to sleep, he
wondered, *Would the Brockles still
be there in the morning?*

Chapter 2

The Wet Shirt

The first sound Bobby heard, even before he opened his eyes, was Groot's voice.

"Murry . . . Murry . . . wake up! Let's get this over with so we can go home."

"What's the rush?" Murry said, yawning and looking at his tiny silver watch. "Bobby's still asleep.

17

Besides, we have to wait until the moon comes out before we can find our way home."

Bobby sat up in bed and stared at the two little men on his pillow. "Are you really going to be here all day?" he asked.

"You bet!" Murry said, hopping onto Bobby's right shoulder. "I'll be sitting here as long as you need me."

"I'll be on your other side,"

Groot said, jumping onto Bobby's left shoulder. "And don't worry about us falling off. We know how to hang on. You can stand on your head and we'll still be here."

Bobby was so excited he bounced out of bed and said, "Wait till I show you to everybody! Wait till Mom and Dad see you! And Abby . . . and Sam!"

Groot laughed, his funny little *heh-heh-heh* laugh and said, "No chance of that, kid."

"What Groot means," Murry explained, "is that you're the only one who can see or hear us."

Bobby didn't believe that. He looked up and saw his mother in

the doorway. She had her hands
on her hips and she was frowning.
"Bobby," she said, "didn't you
hear me? I've been calling and
calling you. It's time to get up."
Bobby didn't say a single

word. He just pointed—first to one shoulder, then to the other.

Mrs. Babbit looked at him and frowned again. "Is there something wrong with your shoulders, dear?" she asked.

"No," said Bobby. Mom didn't see them! They *were* invisible to everyone but him!

"How about getting dressed before you come down," Mrs. Babbit suggested.

"Okay," said Bobby, "but I want my red shirt."

"Now don't start that again," Mrs. Babbit said sternly. "I just washed that shirt yesterday and it's still damp."

"So what? I'll wear it anyway."

"No, you won't."

"Why not?"

"Because I don't want you wearing a wet shirt," Mother said, "and that's that."

Bobby felt Groot tugging on his ear. "Don't let her do this to you," Groot said. "Throw yourself on the floor and kick and scream 'I want it, I want it, I want it, I want it NOW!!!' "

Bobby threw himself down and

pounded the floor with his fists. *"I want it!!!"* he yelled with all his might.

Mrs. Babbit glared at him. "Now you're being unreasonable!" she said angrily.

Murry shook his head. "This isn't working, Groot."

"Okay, I have a better idea," said Groot. "Call her names. Tell her she's mean and that you hate her. Then threaten her. Tell her if she doesn't let you wear that shirt, you won't eat breakfast. Tell her you'll hold your breath until you turn blue. You'll see, she'll give in."

"I doubt it," said Murry, "but

if she does, she'll end up being even madder."

"So what's *your* great advice?" sneered Groot.

"Bobby," said Murry gently, "just tell your mother how you feel. Tell her how much you like that shirt. Then ask her if *she* has any ideas for getting it dry. Then see if *you* have any ideas. You never know what two people can come up with when they try to solve a problem together."

Bobby thought about Murry's words. And then about Groot's words. He had to decide. He didn't want his mother to be mad at him again. He stood up and said, "Gee

Mom, I really wanted to wear my red shirt. It's my favorite. Can you help me think of some way to get it dry fast?"

Mrs. Babbit could hardly believe her own ears. Slowly she repeated Bobby's question. "How can we get your shirt dry fast? . . . The dryer is broken . . . and we can't hang it outside because it's still raining."

Bobby had an idea. "I know! Put it in the oven." And then another. "Put it on the radiator." And then another. "Hang it in front of the fan and let the breeze dry it."

"Hmmm," said Mother. "Your ideas are giving me ideas. We could blow-dry it with my hair dryer. Or I could iron it dry."

"Which is fastest?" Bobby asked.

"Ironing, probably," said his mother. "But then you'll have to wait for breakfast."

"I'll make my own breakfast," Bobby offered.

"It's a deal," said Mrs. Babbit

with a big smile, and she went to
get the ironing board.

Murry jumped up and down.
Puffs of colored smoke came out
of his hat. "You did it!" he
shouted. "You did it! You told
your mother how you felt. And the

two of you came up with ideas.
You worked it out together!"

Groot stamped his foot.
"Dumb luck," he muttered. "I still
think you should have listened to
me, Bobby."

But Bobby wasn't listening to
anyone. He dressed quickly—
except for his shirt—and hurried
down the stairs thinking about
what he would make himself for
breakfast.

28

Chapter 3

"Abby, I'm Mad!"

"Good morning!" said Mr. Babbit, looking up from his Sunday paper as Bobby entered the kitchen. "We were wondering where you were. We just finished breakfast."

"I'm making my own breakfast this morning," Bobby said proudly. Suddenly he noticed his sister. She was sitting at the table drawing

pictures of flowers and she was
using *his* colored pencils—the
pencils Grandpa had bought him!
He snatched them away from her.
Abby snatched them back.

"Don't let her get away with
that!" Groot said. "Kick her in the
shins, bop her on the head, push

30

her off the chair, punch her
in the stomach!"

Bobby took a step closer to
Abby, raised his right hand, and
made a fist. Suddenly he felt Murry
running down his arm. "Stop!
Stop!" Murry shouted. "You can't
do that to your sister."

"Why not?" Groot asked.

31

"Because it's wrong to hurt people!" Murry insisted. "You have to use words. Not kicks or fists or punches."

"I've got some great words," Groot said. "Pest, robber, dummy, jerk, nerd, creep, warthog."

"Groot," Murry said, "you know those words will hurt his sister's feelings."

"So what?" said Groot. "She took his pencils!"

"That's still no reason to call her names," said Murry. "Why can't he ask her to give back his pencils in a pleasant way?"

"Because he's not *feeling* pleasant," said Groot. "The kid is boiling. He's all riled up."

Murry slapped his forehead. "Blazing stars!" he exclaimed. "You're right. Okay, Bobby let's start again. Tell your sister how you feel. Tell her exactly what it is that you don't like."

Slowly Bobby let his hand drop to his side. He thought for a minute. Then he said, "Abby, I'm mad! I don't like it when you take my pencils."

Abby looked up from her coloring. Mr. Babbit looked up from his newspaper. Mrs. Babbit looked up from her ironing. They all looked at Bobby.

"Marvelous!" said Murry. "Now tell her what you *would* like."

"I'd like you to *ask* when you want to use my things."

Murry twirled in the air like a top. A burst of silver bubbles flew

out of his hat. "That's it!" he shouted. "That's it!"

Mr. Babbit stared at Bobby. Mrs. Babbit stared at Bobby. Abby stared at Bobby and said, "Oh . . . okay. But could I just have the red pencil . . . please?"

"No, the red is my favorite," Bobby said, "but you can use one of the other colors—if you give it back."

"Thanks," said Abby, "you're nice," and she picked out a pink pencil and started coloring the flowers.

Once again Mrs. Babbit could hardly believe her ears. "I like the way you handled that, Bobby," she said.

Mr. Babbit said, "I must say, I'm impressed."

"I'm *very* impressed," said Murry.

"I'm sick," said Groot. "Can we go home now?"

Chapter 4

"Don't Go, Sam"

The doorbell rang. It was Sam.
He wanted to be friends again.
Bobby ate some cereal quickly, put
on his red shirt, and went upstairs
with Sam to play.

Sam opened Bobby's closet
and looked inside.

"Let's make a skyscraper,"
Sam said, pulling out the box with
Bobby's construction set and
dumping the pieces onto the floor.

Suddenly Bobby had an idea. A great idea! "We could make a spaceship," he said.

Sam shook his head. "No, I want to make a skyscraper."

"A spaceship is better," Bobby insisted.

Sam shook his head again. "No, a skyscraper is better."

"No, spaceship."

"No, skyscraper."

"Space!"

"Sky!"

Bobby could feel himself getting angry again. Sam always wanted to do the same old thing and he always wanted his own way. Bobby didn't know what to do. Groot tapped his shoulder. "You don't have to listen to him," he hissed. "Why should you do what Sam says? It's your construction set. You're the boss."

Murry opened his mouth to speak.

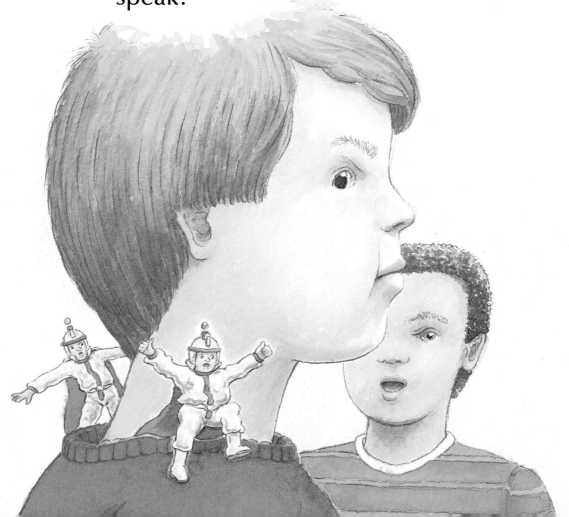

"Now don't you go interfering again," Groot warned him. "This time listen to *me*, kid. Tell Sam it's *your* house and *your* toys and he has to do what *you* say."

Bobby stood up and folded his arms. "Sam," he announced, "this is my house and my toys and you have to do what I say."

Sam stood up and folded his arms. "No, I don't," he protested. "I'm going home."

"Let him," said Groot. "Don't give in. Say, 'Who cares? . . . go home . . . good riddance to bad rubbish. I don't want to be your friend anymore.'"

Murry's face turned bright red. "Bobby," he said, "that's no way to treat a friend. You can't just boss him around and make him do what you want. You have to hear what *he* wants, too. Maybe you can compromise."

"What's 'compromise'?" Bobby asked.

Murry scratched his head,

thinking about how to explain it. "Sometimes you do what you like and sometimes you do what the other person likes . . . . Or sometimes you think up a whole new idea that you'll both like. The trick is for the two of you to try to figure out something that's good for both of you."

Bobby wondered if he and Sam could compromise. He really didn't want Sam to go home. He really did want to be his friend. He said, "Sam, wait. Don't go. We'll do both. We'll make a skyscraper *and* a spaceship.

Sam looked at him suspiciously. Then he said, "But

can we make a skyscraper first?"

"Sure," Bobby agreed, and
they both began to pick out the
biggest pieces for their project.

"Now look what you did,
Murry!" Groot said. "They're
making a skyscraper! Bobby lost.
Sam won. He's getting his way."

"Groot," said Murry, "didn't you see what I saw? Bobby didn't lose. Sam didn't win. He did *not* get his way. Both boys got their way. They worked out a compromise. And that's the best way."

"Wrong, wrong, wrong," said Groot pointing his finger at Murry.

"You think you're smart.
You think you're wise.
You tell the kids to compromise.
I say you're nuts.
I say I'm right.
I say the fun is in the fight."

Groot was so pleased with his

poem, he stood on his head and
kicked his heels in the air.

"Maybe fun for you," said
Murry grinning good-naturedly,
"but I'd rather play than fight. How
about a game of checkers?" He
pulled a tiny silver checkerboard
from under his cape and leaped to
the top of Bobby's dresser.

45

"Okay," said Groot, reaching into his pocket for the checkers, "but I get to go first," and the two Brockles sat cross-legged on the dresser and played checkers while Bobby and Sam made a skyscraper

and then a spaceship that would come down and land on top of the skyscraper.

Chapter 5

The Brockles Say Good-bye

That night after Bobby was tucked into bed, he lay quietly in his dark room, watching the Brockles who had fallen asleep and remembering all that had happened during the day. Suddenly Murry opened his eyes. "Look," he said, shaking Groot gently and pointing to the beam of moonlight that was streaming in through the open window. "We can leave now." Then he put on his cape and turned to Bobby. "Well, that's it, my young friend. Time for us to go."

"Don't go," said Bobby.

"Why not?" asked Murry.

" 'Cause I need you," said Bobby.

"Nah," said Murry, "you don't need us anymore. You know how to get along with your family and friends now. You know the big secret."

"I do?" said Bobby.

"Sure you do," said Murry, motioning him to come closer.

Then he stood on tiptoe and whispered right into Bobby's ear.

48

"When two people disagree
Each other's side they need
to see.
Each needs to think,
What can I do
That's good for me
And good for you?"

Then with one jump he landed
on the beam of moonlight and

started walking toward the
window.

"Hey," said Groot, climbing
onto the moonbeam and running
to catch up to Murry. "Wait for
me! Bye-bye, Bobby!"

Bobby raced to the window.
"Come back, Brockles!" he cried
out. The Brockles paused and
turned around.

"Bobby," said Groot impatiently, "we have a long hike ahead of us. We can't just hang around and talk."

"But I want to give you something," said Bobby, bending down and picking up his spaceship. "Here," he said, holding it out to them with both hands, "you can ride home."

"That's very kind of you," said Murry, "but—"

"I know what you're going to say," Groot interrupted. " 'We shouldn't ride. We both need the exercise. We sit around too much.' But, Murry, it'll be so cool! It'll be such fun! Let's do it!"

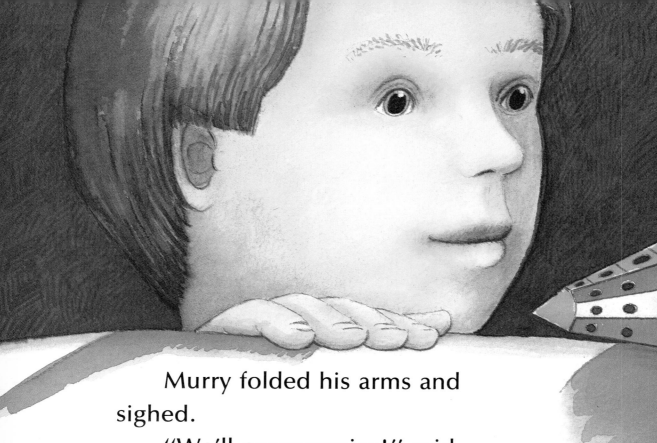

Murry folded his arms and sighed.

"We'll compromise!" said Groot. "We'll ride back in Bobby's spaceship and we'll exercise when we get home. How about it?"

Slowly Murry walked down the moonbeam and inspected Bobby's spaceship. "Interesting design, tight seams, plenty of room . . .

Bobby, are you sure you want to give this to us?"

Bobby nodded his head.

"Okay!" said Groot hopping aboard and pulling Murry inside. "What are we waiting for? Let's go!" Then in a shower of silver sparks the spaceship took off for the Brocklesphere.

"So long, Bobby," he heard the Brockles call out. "This is great! Thanks a lot!"

"Thank *you*!" Bobby called back, but he wasn't sure they heard him, because they were already so far away.

Bobby watched the spaceship grow smaller and smaller until it was just a tiny dot of light, and then it disappeared completely into the starry sky. For the longest time he stood there, staring at the clouds drifting like smoke across the round, silvery moon, and he wondered if he would ever see the Brockles again.